Raintree is an imprint of Capstone Global Library Limited, a company incorporated in England and Wales having its
registered office at 264 Banbury Road, Oxford, OX2 7DY – Registered company number: 6695582

www.raintree.co.uk
myorders@raintree.co.uk

Edited by Chris Harbo
Designed by Brann Garvey and Hilary Wacholz
Production by Kathy McColley
Originated by Capstone Global Library Ltd
Printed and bound in India

ISBN 978 1 4747 7327 0
22 21 20 19
10 9 8 7 6 5 4 3 2

British Library Cataloguing in Publication Data
A full catalogue record for this book is available from the British Library.

TEEN TITANS GO!™

SHOLLY FISCH   MERRILL HAGAN
WRITERS

JORGE CORONA
ARTIST

JEREMY LAWSON
COLOURIST

WES ABBOTT
LETTERER

DAN HIPP
COVER ARTIST

raintree
a Capstone company — publishers for children

5

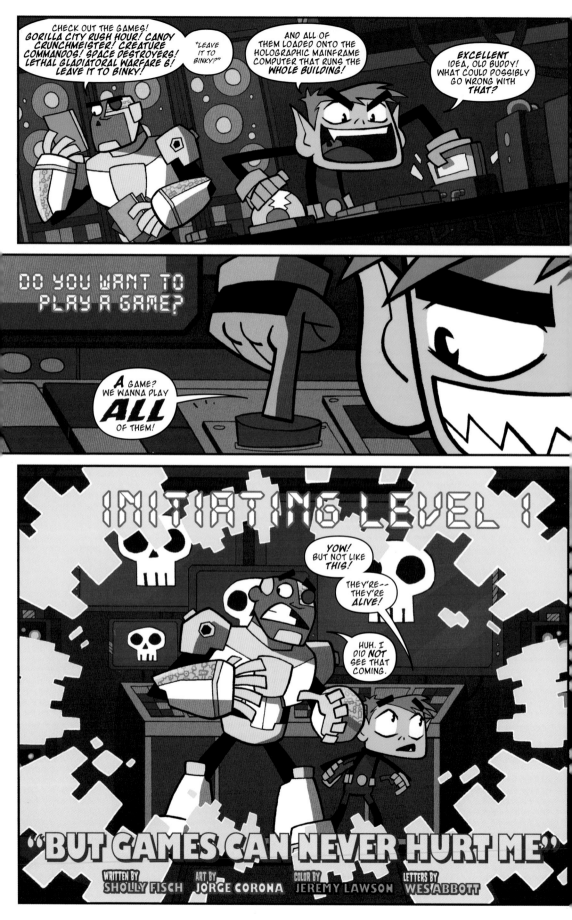

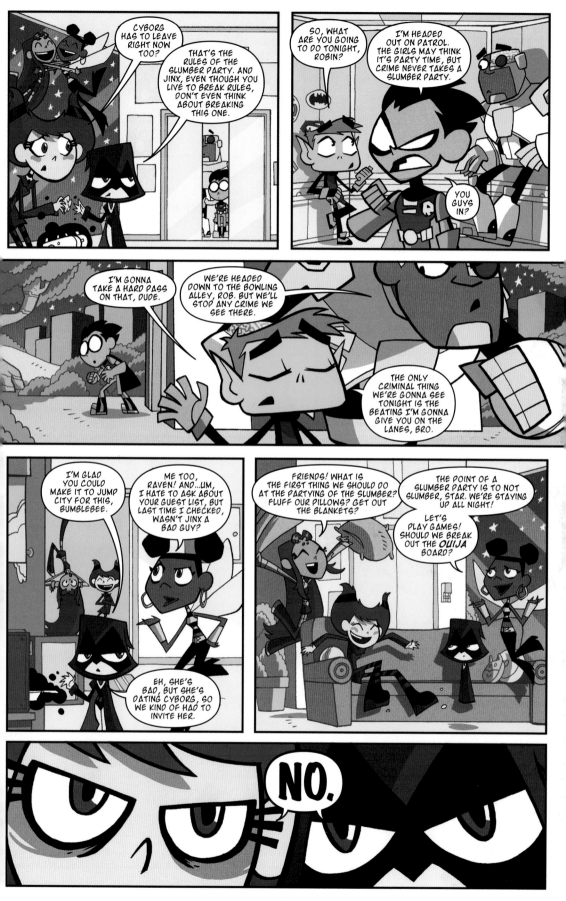

17

20

CREATORS

SHOLLY FISCH

Bitten by a radioactive typewriter, Sholly Fisch has spent the wee hours writing books, comics, TV scripts and online material for over 25 years. His comic book credits include more than 200 stories and features about characters such as Batman, Superman, Bugs Bunny, Daffy Duck, Spider-Man and Ben 10. Currently, he writes stories for Action Comics every month, plus stories for Looney Tunes and Scooby-Doo. By day, Sholly is a mild-mannered developmental psychologist who helps to create educational TV programmes, websites and other media for kids.

MERRILL HAGAN

Merrill Hagan is a writer who has worked on numerous episodes of the hit *Teen Titans Go!* TV show. In addition, he has written several *Teen Titans Go!* comic books and was a writer for the original *Teen Titans* series in 2003.

JORGE CORONA

Jorge Corona is a Venezuelan comic book artist who is well known for his all-ages fantasy-adventure series *Feathers* and his work on *Jim Henson's The Storyteller: Dragons*. In addition to *Teen Titans Go!*, he has also worked on *Batman Beyond*, *Justice League Beyond*, *We Are Robin*, *Goners* and many other comics.

GLOSSARY

conquer defeat and take control of an enemy

dimension realm of existence

distract draw attention away from something

employ use something

holographic having to do with an image made by laser beams that looks three-dimensional

interface point at which two different things meet

irritated annoyed or angry

mainframe large and very powerful computer

meditate relax the mind and body using regular mental exercises

menace threat or danger

patrol action of watching and protecting a particular area

placid calm or peaceful

pursue follow or chase someone in order to catch him or her

random without any order or purpose

recurring happening again

server large and powerful computer that connects other computers in a network

spirit soul or invisible part of a person that is believed to control thoughts and feelings

starch substance that comes from foods such as potatoes and wheat. When made into a powder, starch can be used to stiffen clothing.

sufficient enough or adequate amount

summon call or request someone to come

VISUAL QUESTIONS & WRITING PROMPTS

1. Why did the illustrator include character icons on the left and right sides of this panel? What do they make you think of?

2. The video game characters power up at the end of the first story. What happens next? Write a short story about how the Teen Titans defeat them again.

3. Based on this panel, how successful were the girls at piercing Starfire's ears? Explain why you think so.

4. What does this panel tell you about Cyborg's method of bowling? Is his approach fair to Beast Boy? Why or why not?